First published in Great Britain in 1998 by
Macdonald Young Books
an imprint of Wayland Publishers Ltd
61 Western Road
Hove
East Sussex
BN3 1JD

Text copyright © Jana Novotny Hunter 1998
Illustrations copyright © Sue Porter 1998

Find Macdonald Young Books on the internet at http://www.myb.co.uk

Printed and bound in Portugal by Edições ASA
British Library Cataloguing in Publication Data available.

ISBN: 0 7500 2282 5

A big bearhug to our dear
friend Anne Plenderleith
from Jana and Sue

MACDONALD YOUNG BOOKS

A Bearhug at Bedtime

Psst!
Tiger!

Jana Novotny Hunter · Sue Porter

In the jungle, there is a tiger.
A stripey, yellow tiger . . .

hiding behind trees,
chasing you through tall grasses –
ready to *pounce!*

Run, run, *run!*

Over under and through.

But . . .

. . . if he's quick and catches you
(as tigers do in the end) . . .

. . . stroke his ears and cuddle him.
He just wants to be your friend.

In a tower there's a dragon,
a fiery, green dragon . . .

waiting to be freed,
roaring and snorting fire,
his eyes *flashing*.

Fly, fly, *fly* him far.

Free him from the spell.

But . . .

. . . if your ride home makes him sleepy
(it won't take very long) . . .

. . . tuck him up snug and sing to him,
a dragon's bedtime song.

In the mountains there's a bear.
A hairy-beary bear . . .

who bounds out from nowhere,
snapping at your heels,
growling at you.

Climb, climb, climb

up the mountain fast.

But . . .

. . . if he saves you from a fall

(make sure you hold on tight)

. . . then show him he's the best bear of all and give him a bearhug goodnight!

Goodnight!